World of Reading

STAR WARS™

AT-AT ATTACK!

WRITTEN BY CALLIOPE GLASS

ART BY PILOT STUDIO

PRESS

Los Angeles • New York

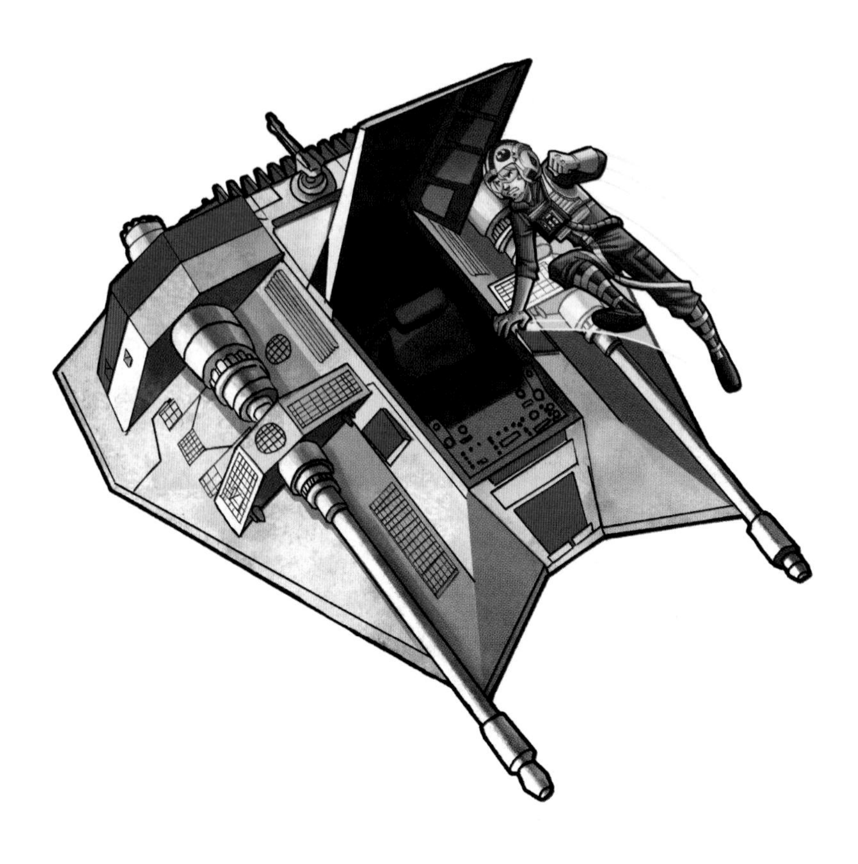

For information address Disney • Lucasfilm Press, 1200 Grand Central Avenue, Glendale, California 91201.

Printed in China

First Boxed Set Edition, October 2016 10 9 8 7

Library of Congress Control Number on file

FAC-025393-22178

ISBN 978-1-4847-9035-9

Visit the official *Star Wars* website at: www.starwars.com.

The planet Hoth
was very, very cold.
Nobody wanted
to live there.

It was the perfect place
for Luke, Han, Leia,
and the rebel army
to hide.

They were hiding
from Darth Vader.

Vader sent robots into
space to find
the secret rebel base.
One of the robots found it.

Vader sent his AT-ATs
to attack the rebels.
The rebel base was
not safe anymore.

Princess Leia
told all the rebels
to fly away.

But she chose to leave last
to make sure the rebels
left safely. Han and C-3PO
stayed with her.

Luke wanted to
protect the base.
The rebels needed
time to escape.

Luke hopped into
a fast ship.

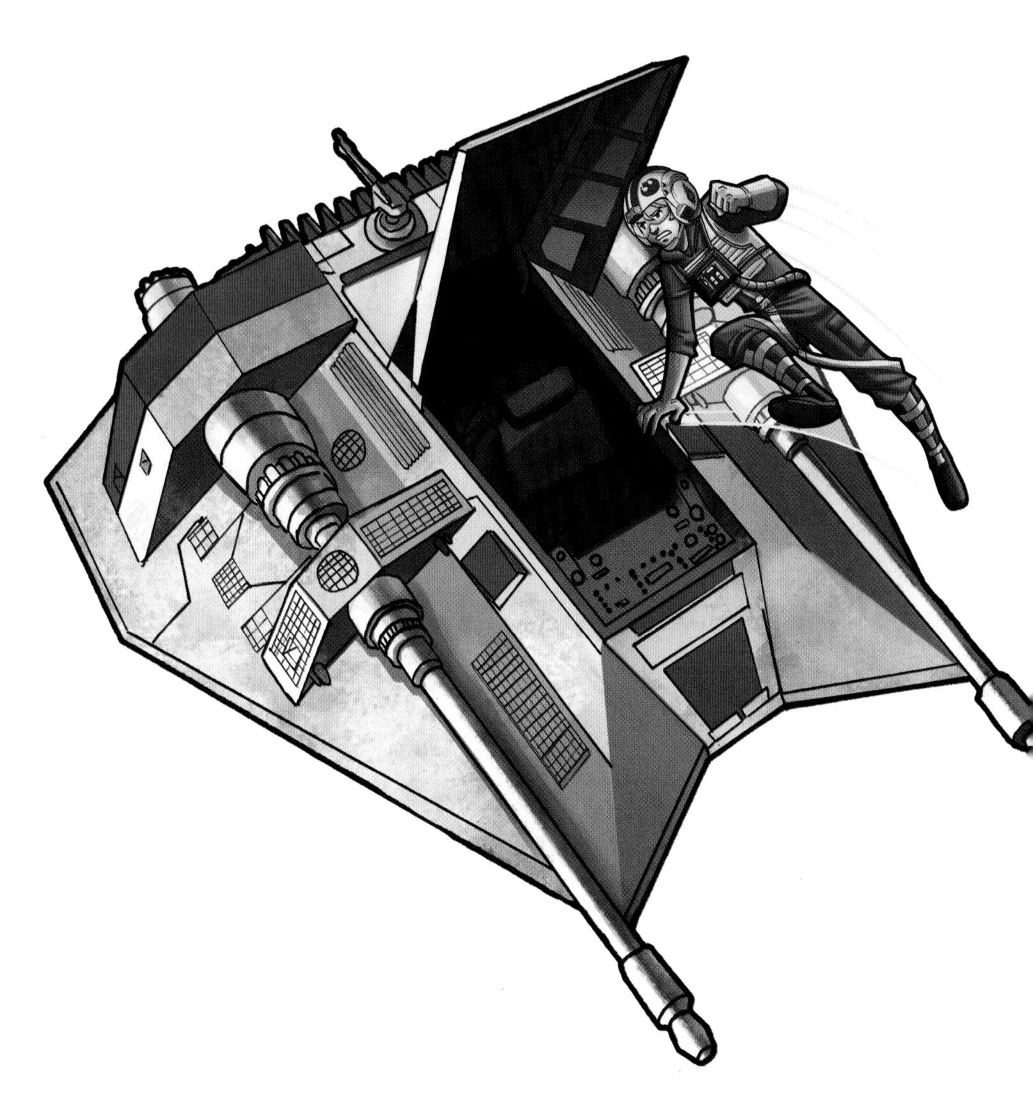

He flew out
to attack the AT-ATs.

The AT-ATs were strong.
Luke tried shooting at them,
but nothing happened.

While Luke fought the AT-ATs,
Han, Leia, and C-3PO
ran to Han's ship.

But Han's ship was not working.
The motor would not start.

Leia was annoyed.
She thought Han's ship
was a bucket of bolts.

Han and his friend Chewie
tried to fix the ship.

They were running
out of time.

Luke needed to
stop the AT-ATs.

Luke and his friends
used cables to trip an AT-AT.

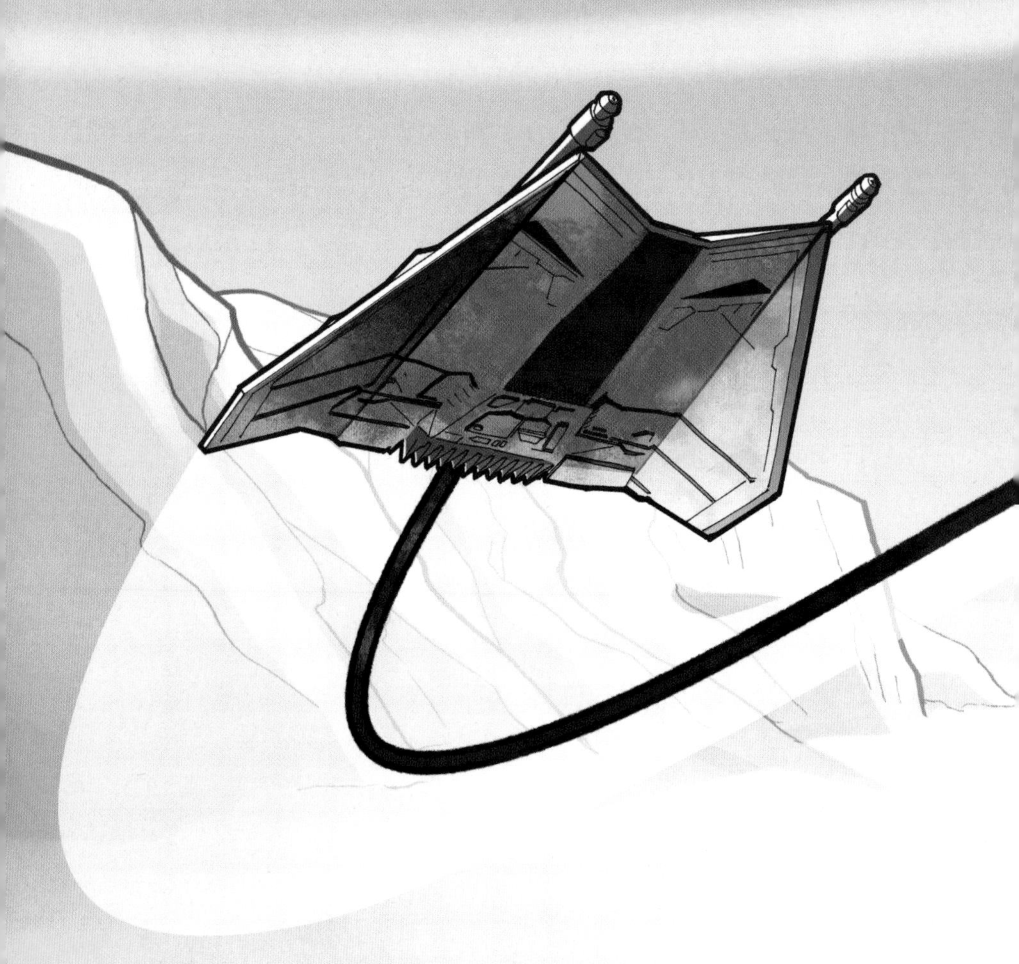

The AT-AT fell down.
Then it exploded!

Luke used his lightsaber
to stop another AT-AT.

Luke had saved the day!

Darth Vader arrived at the base.

Vader and his troops
fired at Han's ship.

But at the very last minute . . .

. . . Han's ship
finally started.

Han and Leia flew away.
Luke saw their ship escape.
Luke smiled.
They were all safe!

Their base was destroyed,
but the rebels had
escaped to fight another day.